Escape the
AVALANCHE

Steph

GW00729221

MENTOR

This Edition first published 1999 by

MENTOR PRESS
43 Furze Road,
Sandyford Industrial Estate,
Dublin 18.

Tel. (01) 295 2112/3   Fax. (01) 295 2114
e-mail: mentor1@indigo.ie

ISBN: 1-902586-49-2

A catalogue record for this book is available from the
British Library

Cover Illustration: Nicola Sedgwick
Typesetting, editing, design and layout by Mentor Press

Printed in Ireland by ColourBooks

1 3 5 7 9 10 8 6 4 2

CONTENTS

The Author

Stephanie Dagg

Stephanie Dagg lives in Innishannon, County Cork.

She is married to Chris and is mother of two children, Benjamin and Caitlín, and has been writing stories ever since she was a child. Originally from Suffolk in England, she moved to Cork in 1992.

Dedicated to Chris

'Love is the only gold'
TENNYSON

1 Back in France

'Wow! What an awesome view!'

Tom Donoghue, his little sister Anna, his Mum and his best friend Kevin Murphy stood at the window of their apartment in the French ski resort of Grandmont. They were looking across a vast expanse of deep snow to the mountains beyond, which were dominated by the huge mass of Mont Glace. Everything glowed in the late evening sun.

It was Tom who had broken the hushed silence as they gazed in wonder at the sight. It was a far cry from grey old Cork!

'Mega!' breathed Kevin.

'Lovely!' sighed Mum. She sat down in front of the window, exhausted from a long day of travelling. She was dying for a cup of tea and she was well aware that in a moment she must start unpacking. But just for now she couldn't tear herself away from the wonderful sight of snowy mountains. Three-year-old Anna snuggled sleepily into her lap. It was all a bit much for her.

'Alan was right when he said it was nice here,' said Tom, sitting down next to Mum. 'When's he arriving, Mum?'

'Three days' time,' replied Mum, happily.

They had met Alan, who was a scientist, on holidays in the summer in the Auvergne. That had been quite a holiday as a nearby dormant volcano had erupted, leading to a very exciting adventure for Mum and the children. Alan had since become a great friend of the family.

To make up for having their summer holiday cut short so spectacularly, Mum was now treating them all to a winter holiday. She'd invited Alan to join them and he'd suggested that they come here to Grandmont. He was due to arrive as soon as term finished at the University where he was a professor. He had booked an apartment close to theirs.

'I don't ever want to move!' said Tom. He just couldn't get over the sight of all the snow.

'We'll be able to build some ginormous snowmen!' grinned Kevin.

'Yeah, a whole army of them!' agreed Tom. 'And there'd still be enough snow left for another zillion.'

Mum groaned and lifted Anna off her lap.

'Come on, gang, I'm starving. Let's just unpack the necessities for now and head off into town. How about it?'

'Will there be a McDonald's?' asked Kevin hopefully. It was his first question wherever they went on holidays.

Mum rolled up her eyes in mock despair. 'I expect so. There always is!'

'Goodie!' shouted Anna, perking up. 'Chips, chips, I want chips!'

'Me too. Tons of them,' added Tom.

'Well, come on then, let's get going!' urged Mum, her hopes of a nice authentic French meal dashed.

The boys scampered around the apartment. There was a large kitchen-cum-living room with three bedrooms leading from it and a rather small bathroom complete with shower, basin and bidet.

'Not one of those things again!' groaned Kevin when he saw it. He wasn't impressed with bidets!

'Which room will we pick?' asked Tom. 'This one's got the best view. It looks towards Mont Glace.'

'Maybe we should let your Mum have it, then,' said Kevin, considerately.

'Yeah, that would be nice,' agreed Tom. 'So come on, then. Which one should we take?'

There wasn't much to choose between the other two rooms. They were practically identical, being very small with twin beds. One offered a marginally nicer view of a distant pine forest, so the boys opted for that.

They dragged their suitcases in and unpacked. Well, Kevin unpacked, carefully putting his shirts and trousers in the wardrobe and his jumpers in the chest of drawers. Tom did his usual trick of tipping his case out into a corner of the room.

'You're crazy, Tom. You know that your Mum'll go nuts!' protested Kevin.

'No, she won't!' grinned Tom. 'This holiday is a special treat. She won't care.'

But Tom was wrong. Mum *did* care and she made Tom put his clothes away properly. Tom grumbled at Mum, and Kevin grumbled at Tom because he was holding them all up and Kevin was starving.

'That's better,' said Mum eventually when the floor was clear of clothes again. 'Come on, let's go and eat!'

2 Grandmont

It was another five minutes before they left the apartment. There were so many layers of clothes to put on! It was much, much colder than anything they had ever known back home in Ireland. Even with two pairs of gloves, a hat, a scarf, a body warmer under a padded jacket and big padded moon boots, the boys and Anna felt chilly to start with. Poor Mum felt frozen!

'Oh, I hate the cold!' she gasped when the frozen evening air hit them as they stepped out of the cosy apartment building. 'Whatever made me want to bring you lot on a winter holiday?'

'You love us, Mrs D!' said Kevin. 'That's why!'

'Huh, you reckon?' teased Mum. She clapped her hands together in their big thick mittens and stamped her feet as she and the children shuffled through the snow, which was deep and crisp. The pine trees all around them were frosted with snow and ice. Millions of stars twinkled in a clear sky and a bright full moon shone down, casting long shadows of the trees on the glistening snow.

'Lovely!' exclaimed Anna.

'Yeah, not bad!' agreed Tom.

'Yes, it's *very* not bad,' sighed Mum happily. 'It's worth all the chilblains I'll get.'

'You're just a lizard, Mum,' Tom pointed out.

'Cor, you should wallop him for being so rude, Mrs D!' protested Kevin.

'No, it's true!' laughed Mum. 'I've always got cold hands and feet.'

'Cold blooded, you see, just like a lizard!' Tom explained.

'Tom and his Dad used to tease me about it,' Mum went on. 'They had a pet name for me. Actually, Kevin, it was the name of a dinosaur – Maiasaurus.'

'What does that mean?' asked Kevin puzzled. 'I know Tyrannosaurus Rex means "king of the dinosaurs" or something, but I've never heard of mayo . . . meow . . . whatever.'

'Maiasaurus means "good mother lizard",' explained Tom. 'The Maiasaurs looked after each other's eggs, or so the experts think from studying the fossils. That's why they thought they were good mothers. And our Mum's a good mother – but she's a lizard too!'

'Well, I still think Tom and his Dad were very rude,' retorted Kevin indignantly. 'I'd never call you a lizard, Mrs D, not in a trillion years.'

'Thank you,' laughed Mum, giving Kevin a hug. 'Ooh, aren't you warm. I'm not letting go of you now.'

They tramped happily down the snow-covered path towards the small town of Grandmont, laughing and messing around. Tom felt really, really happy, mainly because Mum was really, really happy. What a difference from even just a few months ago when Mum had been sad nearly all the time, although she had pretended not to be. It had taken Mum a long time to get over Dad's death. It had taken Tom and Anna a long time too, but he could see that it had been much harder for Mum. She'd been left, not only with the heartache, but with two young children to bring up. Anna had been just a baby when Dad died.

But since Mum had met Alan, she'd really started to cheer up. Mum hadn't liked Alan at first, but during their volcano adventure in the summer, they'd become close friends. Tom, Anna and Kevin all liked Alan too. He lived in England but he'd been over to visit them a few times in Cork.

Kevin told Tom that Alan might be his new Dad. Tom wasn't sure what he thought about that – but now wasn't the time to worry about it, he decided. He happily scooped up a huge lump of snow and lobbed it at Kevin. Kevin ducked and the snowball hit Mum who started to chase Tom. They charged around like hooligans until they reached the edge of the town.

'Come along, now!' panted Mum, brushing snow out of her eyes and off her hat. 'Time to behave like human beings again. We're back in civilisation.'

'Boring!' moaned Tom.

'Maybe,' smiled Mum. 'But civilisation also means McDonald's and look what I can see . . .'

Sure enough, at the end of the first street, there it was, bright and snug.

'Yippee!' cheered Kevin. 'Last one there's a sissy!' and the three children tore off towards it. Mum trotted along behind, chuckling to see them all enjoying themselves so much.

'This,' she thought to herself, 'is going to be a nice, normal holiday – our best ever!'

3 Skiing

The next day was beautiful. The sky was clear and blue and the sun was shining.

'Go away, rotten sun!' moaned Kevin when he opened the curtains and saw it.

'Why?' yawned Tom. 'It's nice to see the sun in the middle of winter.'

'Yeah, but it'll melt all the snow and we haven't built any snowmen yet,' Kevin pointed out.

'Silly banana, the snow won't melt that quickly. It's still freezing cold outside anyway.' Tom said this as he scuttled across the bare wooden floor of their bedroom to the bathroom. He'd forgotten his slippers, even though Mum had reminded him at least twenty times to pack them. His feet were like blocks of ice within seconds.

The boys got dressed quickly, then went into the kitchen where Mum was getting breakfast ready with Anna's help. Tom's mouth watered as he smelt some fresh, warm croissants.

'Yum, where did you get the croissants, Mum?' he asked, jumping onto one of the chairs at the table.

'A baker's van came round earlier,' replied Mum. 'He even had some pots of homemade jam too, so prepare yourself for a feast!'

She pulled a loaded baking tray out of the oven and placed it on the table with a flourish. Silence reigned for the next ten minutes as everyone concentrated on eating. Soon only a few flakes of pastry and some very sticky fingers were all that remained.

'Delicious!' sighed Kevin, licking the jam off his thumb. 'What are we doing today, Mrs D?'

'Well, I thought we'd get you two started with skiing lessons. Anna's too small so we'll go exploring while you two hit the piste,' said Mum.

'Oh no, I can hardly move after all that breakfast,' groaned Kevin. 'I'll never be able to ski!'

'Serves you right, greedy guts!' said Tom unsympathetically. He was a bit annoyed because Kevin had pinched the last croissant just as he himself had been about to take it. 'Aren't you going skiing, Mum?'

'Yes, when Alan's here. He can mind Anna for me so I can have a go. It's something I've never done and I'd love to try.' Mum looked really excited. Tom was pleased to see her so happy.

'Come on, guys!' she said, getting up. 'Help me clear away and then we'll head for the ski school.'

The ski school had an office in a small wooden chalet next to the ski slopes. It was packed, even though they got there just after it opened. When it was their turn, Mum put the boys' names down for beginners' lessons. They were told to hire boots and skis in the next chalet and then to meet on the nursery slope at ten o'clock.

'Nursery slope?' spluttered Tom, indignantly. 'We're not babies!'

But a few minutes after ten, standing at the top of the nursery slope and looking down, Tom felt terrified. The nursery slope looked enormous! Tom felt like he was at the top of the ski jump he'd seen on the Winter Olympics on TV. This skiing business was quite a challenge, Tom thought.

Kevin was quiet too. He felt very awkward in his large clumpy ski boots. Tom had been first to put boots on and Kevin had roared with laughter as his friend stumbled around in them, his knees bent and his bottom sticking out. But then Kevin had put his on and realised how difficult it was to walk in them. And his skis looked huge. They seemed to stretch on for ever in front of him.

What made things worse was the fact that Tom and Kevin were the oldest and biggest in their class. Some of the kids with them were tiny, easily younger than Anna. Mum saw the boys' glowering faces and chuckled quietly.

Just then the ski instructor arrived and introduced herself as Yvette. In no time at all, she had them learning the *chasse-neige,* or snowplough position, and they began sliding around on their skis. Kevin was surprised to find it really easy. OK, it made his legs ache a bit but he didn't fall over once. Yvette kept telling him how well he was doing.

Tom, on the other hand, was hopeless. He just couldn't get the hang of his skis at all. Every time he tried to stop, he just fell flat on his face. Soon his mittens and trousers were soaking wet and his ankles and knees ached too. He was not impressed with skiing at all!

At last the lesson finished.

'Oh, is that it?' asked Kevin disappointed. 'Shame. That was mega. What did you think, Tom?'

Kevin had been so engrossed in skiing that he hadn't noticed how badly Tom had been getting on.

Tom pulled a face. 'Skiing stinks!' he growled, and stomped off to take his skis back.

Kevin shrugged and grinned. 'I guess you didn't enjoy it then!' he shouted at his friend's back and then hurried to catch him up. He'd got something to tease Tom about now!

4 The Altiport

Tom's bad mood didn't last too long. Mum and Anna had been shopping while the boys were at skiing class and had bought them some French football gear, as well as vast quantities of delicious looking food. Then halfway through lunch Mum sprang her surprise.

'Shall we go and see the altiport after dinner?' she asked casually.

'What's an altiport, Mrs D?' asked Kevin in a rather muffled voice as his mouth was full of pasta.

'It's an airport,' Mum explained.

'An airport?' echoed Tom. 'But there isn't an airport near here, is there? We're miles away from any big cities.'

Kevin looked intrigued too.

'There's one here at this resort!' announced Mum, her eyes twinkling. 'An altiport is a small airport on a mountain. It's for private planes only,' she explained. 'But the one here is quite busy. There were a lot of planes taking off from there this morning. I'm surprised you didn't notice them.'

'I was whizzing along too fast to see anything!' boasted Kevin.

'And all I got to see was snow!' laughed Tom. He was beginning to see the funny side of his disastrous attempt at skiing. 'I can't wait to see the planes, Mum.' Tom loved planes.

The children finished their meal in double quick time.

'Come on, let's go!' said Kevin.

They set off up a winding road that took them into the hills above Grandmont. They seemed to be walking into the middle of nowhere but suddenly a light aircraft buzzed into the sky above them. It was very low.

'Look!' called Tom. 'That plane has just taken off. We must be nearly there!'

Kevin and Tom raced ahead. They rounded a corner – and there was the altiport. It didn't look much like an airport to the boys. There was just a couple of small buildings, a very short runway – and lots of snow! A few brightly coloured small planes were parked beside the runway. And that was it.

'Look at the red plane!' cried Anna.

'Wow! What a weird airport!' said Kevin.

'Not weird really,' answered Mum. 'Just a mountain one. You can't expect it to look like Cork airport now, can you!'

'But the runway's so short!' Tom pointed out. 'How on earth do the planes manage to take off in that short space? It must be scary!'

They stood and watched the planes for a while. Tom had brought his book about civil aircraft and he and Kevin argued over what type each plane was. The altiport looked quite busy with pilots and mechanics wandering around. A plump, grey-haired man walked up to a plane that Tom said was a Piper Cherokee but Kevin said was a Cessna.

'Well, which is it then?' demanded Tom crossly.

'Let me borrow your book and I'll tell you,' replied Kevin confidently.

Tom handed it over with a grunt, and then went back to watching the man as he walked round his plane. He was checking the flaps by giving each one an energetic heave.

'Golly, is he trying to break them off?' gasped Tom.

'No, he's just checking that everything's safe before he takes off,' said Mum. 'Very wise.'

Next the man peered into the fuel tanks in the wings. After that, he siphoned off a small plastic tube full of fuel from a valve under the wings, inspected it and then threw it away.

'Mummy, he's throwing his petrol away,' Anna pointed out.

'It's not petrol, silly,' Tom butted in. 'Planes use avgas.'

'Well, Anna wouldn't know about that,' Mum pointed out. 'And he's only throwing a bit away. I think he's checking it for . . . Good gracious me!' Mum suddenly exclaimed.

'What is it, Mum?' asked Tom.

'What's he checking for, Mrs D?' asked Kevin, intrigued.

But Mum wasn't listening.

'It isn't, is it? No, it can't be!' she gasped.

'Isn't what?' demanded Tom.

'Good heavens! It is! Well, I never would have thought!' cried Mum.

'What? What?' the children shouted.

'Stay here! I'll be back in a minute!' and with that, Mum nimbly jumped over the fence and trotted towards the man they had been watching.

'Where's Mummy going?' asked Anna.

'*Excusez-moi, monsieur,*' they heard her call, '*mais est-ce que tu es André Lebrun? C'est moi, Jane Kenny.*'

'Kenny? That's not your mum's real name,' protested Kevin.

'It was her name before she married my Dad,' explained Tom. 'But what's she doing?'

They watched in amazement as the man turned round, looked closely at Mum and then suddenly threw his arms open wide and ran up to her. They gave each other a big hug.

'Must be an old boyfriend,' decided Tom.

'And boy, is he an *old* old boyfriend,' grinned Kevin.

Mum and André were deep in conversation. Then Mum pointed over to the children and the two grown-ups wandered over to them. Mum was smiling happily.

'André, I'd like you to meet my two children Tom and Anna and our friend Kevin Murphy.' André smiled and shook hands with them all.

'And this, gang, is Monsieur André Lebrun. I used to be an au pair for his family in Paris more years ago than I care to remember,' Mum explained at last.

'*Mais oui*, my children have all grown up and left home now,' smiled André. 'In fact I now have, oh, how do you say it, grandchilds!'

'I think you mean grandchildren,' Kevin said politely.

'Grandchildren. *Oui, c'est ça!*' agreed André.

Mum and the children chatted away for a few more minutes, telling André about their disastrous summer holiday and then about the fun they were having on this holiday.

'*C'est bon!* But how would you like another adventure? Would you like to come up with me in my Cherokee?' asked André.

'See!' hissed Tom, elbowing Kevin in the ribs. 'Told you it was a Cherokee!'

But Kevin took no notice.

'No kidding! Can we really go up in your plane? Mega zega cool! Can we, Mrs D?' he begged.

'Well,' began Mum doubtfully. 'I'm not sure we'd all fit, would we?'

'It *will* be a bit of a squash if we all go at once. How about I take *les garçons* first, and then I will return for *les filles*?' André suggested.

'But that means you've got to make two trips,' said Mum.

25

'*Pas de problème!*' grinned André. 'I love flying. The more trips the better. OK, *mes petits. Allez!*'

Tom and Kevin could hardly believe their luck! The last thing they'd expected to do today was to go flying in a tiny little plane from an airport halfway up a mountain.

André pulled open the door of the Cherokee and tipped the pilot's seat forward.

'In you get!' he smiled.

Kevin nimbly hopped up onto the wing and squeezed through the doorway onto the back seat. Tom followed him.

'Put on the seatbelts, please' ordered André, 'and then the headsets. You'll be able to listen in to the control tower then.'

'Mad!' grinned Tom happily.

Mum peered in through the door at them a bit anxiously. The plane looked so small and fragile!

'OK?' she asked.

Kevin gave her a thumbs up sign.

'*Maintenant!* Now, I come!' announced André. He had a bit of difficulty heaving himself up on to the wing, and squeezing his bulk through the doorway. He rolled his eyes in mock despair.

'*Oh, là là.* We French like our food too much!' he sighed, sitting down and patting his stomach. 'It is not a good thing for pilots!'

He turned to Mum and Anna.

'We will be back in a little while,' he told them. 'We will just have a quick look at *les belles montagnes.*'

Mum waved at the boys and then stepped back. André pulled the door firmly shut and locked it. Then he strapped himself in, put on his headset and began checking the various dials and displays in front of him. He began a conversation in French over his headphones. The boys listened in eagerly. They couldn't understand what was going on, but it was still fun to hear the conversation.

Then André turned the ignition key and pumped the throttle and the engine sprang into life with a healthy roar. A few more checks and then they began to taxi nimbly forward.

But suddenly they stopped.

'What's up?' cried Tom in alarm. 'Have we broken down?'

'*Non!*' André chuckled. 'I am just testing the brakes. It is *très important.*'

'At least they work,' Tom sighed with relief.

The plane started moving slowly forward again. Tom glanced out of the window and saw Mum and Anna waving madly at them. He waved back.

'OK in the back?' called André above the engine noise.

'You bet!' Kevin called back.

'*Bon*. We will take off in a moment!'

The words 'take off' reminded Tom about the very short runway. Suddenly he stopped feeling quite so excited.

'Er, how long is the runway, André?' he asked.

'It is four hundred metres – enormous!' came the reply.

'It seems to slope down a lot,' remarked Kevin doubtfully, looking out through the windscreen.

'Only about eleven degrees,' called André over his shoulder. 'It just looks more! *Courage!*'

André paused at the start of the runway. He began to mutter to himself.

'Is he praying?' whispered Tom to Kevin.

Kevin shrugged. 'I don't know. Maybe it's a pilot's ritual or something,' he suggested.

André had stopped his muttering. Somehow he must have sensed the boys' puzzlement. 'I was doing my final checks while we wait for clearance.

There are many things a pilot has to check. It is not like driving *une voiture!*'

The voice of the air traffic controller came over the headphones and the boys caught the word '*décollage*' — take off.

'*Eh bien! En route!*' called André.

He pushed the throttle gradually forward and the Cherokee accelerated smoothly and furiously. The boys were amazed at the power. And then suddenly, they were in the air! The land dropped away below them and the runway disappeared. All they could see ahead of them was snow and the rugged peaks of the high mountains.

'Mega!' enthused Kevin.

'What a view, eh?' remarked André, turning slightly to glance round at the boys. As he turned, the whole plane tilted a little. It was sensitive to the slightest shift in weight.

Tom gripped the seat beneath him tightly in a moment of panic. But then as he looked out of the window again at the dramatic sight he relaxed. This is amazing! he thought.

They were flying high above Grandmont now. Tom recognised their block of apartments and Kevin, of course, spotted McDonald's!

André chatted away, pointing out various features in between talking in French over his headphones. The boys caught sight of tiny figures skiing down the slopes beneath them. Then the plane swooped high over a jutting ridge, and on the other side they saw a glistening glacier.

'Cool!' shouted Tom as he watched the plane's shadow racing over the snow below them. 'This is the life!' They flew in a great, wide circle and soon they were facing back towards the altiport.

'We don't want your poor *maman* to worry!' grinned André. 'Perhaps you will come up for a longer flight with me soon?'

'Yes please!' said Kevin.

Tom decided to see what the landing was like before he committed himself. He wasn't looking forward to the touchdown. It wasn't quite as scary as he imagined it would be – but it wasn't far off! The plane seemed to practically nose dive towards the altiport, the descent was so steep. It was also very dramatic as they were heading straight for the mountain! However, André brought them down as lightly as a feather and they soon taxied to a halt.

'*Voilà*!' said the Frenchman.

'Oh wow!' breathed Kevin. 'That was ace! Thanks André, I mean, *merci beaucoup!*'

'*De rien!*' said André. 'It was my pleasure! Now, I must take the girls!'

When the plane had come to a stop, André climbed out and then let the boys out. Now it was Mum and Anna's turn to climb aboard. But Anna had decided that she didn't want to go for a flight after all and Mum didn't seem too disappointed about that. Tom knew that Mum wasn't really very keen on flying.

'*Bien.* Perhaps another day, then?' said André. 'Here is the phone number of our hotel. You must ring us. Evelyn would love to see you, Jane.'

'And I'd love to see her,' said Mum, with a smile. 'Of course I'll phone. But now I must get this lot home for tea. Thanks again André.'

André climbed back into the plane and Mum and the three children waited and watched him take off and disappear into the blue sky.

'What a nice guy!' remarked Kevin.

'It was really fun, Mum,' said Tom.

The two boys told Mum and Anna all about the flight as they trudged back home.

5 Inside a Glacier

Tom woke late the next morning. He heard the others talking in the kitchen.

'I'd better get in there fast,' he muttered to himself, 'or Kev will scoff all the croissants!'

He pushed back the covers and swung his legs out of the bed – or rather started to – but stopped very quickly as a dreadful pain shot up his legs.

'Oww! Oww!' he howled.

The door of the bedroom burst open and Mum rushed in.

'Whatever is it, Tom?' she asked anxiously. 'Are you ill?'

'I can't move,' groaned Tom, as he fell back on the bed. 'My legs are in agony!'

Mum's worried face relaxed into a smile.

'Your muscles are just stiff after skiing, silly!' she grinned. 'Come on, the sooner you get moving the better.'

She disappeared back into the kitchen to sort out an argument over the jam between Anna and Kevin.

Tom hesitated for a moment, and then decided to be brave. He gingerly moved his legs again. Ouch, painful! He started to sit up. Suddenly his stomach muscles gave a twinge.

'Boy, do I hate skiing!' he growled.

Slowly but surely he kept moving and at last he had raised himself into a standing position. He shuffled stiffly into the kitchen.

'Hey, look everyone, it's a robot!' laughed Kevin. 'Morning, Tom!'

Tom scowled.

'Oh, don't be such a crosspatch,' said Mum. 'Come and get some food inside you and you'll feel lots better.'

She pushed a plate of warm croissants towards him. Tom stretched out an aching arm and helped himself. Kevin poured out a mug of tea for his friend and Anna dropped four lumps of sugar in before Mum noticed what she was doing and stopped her. Tom didn't mind, he loved sweet tea.

Sure enough, in a few minutes he did start to feel more cheerful. Everything stopped hurting after a while. Then Kevin admitted that he felt a bit tender too.

'So, no skiing today then?' asked Mum.

The two strained looks she got from the boys answered her question.

'Swimming is very good for sore muscles,' she told them. 'Let's head for the swimming pool this morning.'

Mum was right as usual. After a splash around in the lovely warm pool, both Tom and Kevin felt just about back to normal. They felt hungry too, so they decided to go to McDonald's for a second breakfast. On the way out, in the reception area, they passed a notice board with a large sign which had the heading '*Loisirs*' on it.

'What's this all about then?' wondered Mum, peering at it. 'Oh, it says there's an activity club for kids aged 9 to 13. Look, you can do hikes in the snow and tobogganing and things. Let me see. What date is it today? There's an "eight-kilometre hike with a qualified guide on the 15th, departing from the ski school". That's tomorrow isn't it? "Bring lunch" it says.'

'Mad!' exclaimed Kevin in delight. 'I'd love to go on a hike, wouldn't you, Tom?'

'Yeah. Can we go, Mum?' asked Tom.

'I don't see why not. You have to meet at ten at the ski school. "Get back at about three" it says.

Now that would be handy because Alan arrives tomorrow at one. Anna and I can go and collect him from the station in St Jean de Montagne and we can all meet up at the ski school afterwards. Great, that's tomorrow taken care of.'

'What does this other notice say?' asked Tom. The other notice showed a picture of what looked like an icy cave. As usual all the words were in French and Tom couldn't make them out.

'Let's take another look and see,' said Mum, frowning in concentration as she tried to translate some of the words. '*Grotte ... glacier ... visite ...*' she murmured. 'Hey!' she cried as she deciphered the words. 'It says there's a cave cut into the glacier near here. You can actually walk inside the glacier! "Open every day" it says.'

'Mega!' said Tom. 'Can we all go there now? Kev and I saw the glacier from the air with André yesterday. It looked brilliant.'

'Oh yes! I'd love to go underneath all those millions of tons of ice,' agreed Kevin.

Anna, who had been looking excited, started to look scared at Kevin's words. Mum frowned at him.

'Well, not millions of tons, Anna – er, just a few really,' he added lamely.

'It's OK, Anna,' said Mum, lifting Anna up. 'Remember the caves you and the boys explored in the summer when you were escaping from the volcano?' Anna nodded. 'Well, this cave is like those ones – strong and safe, except it's carved out of ice instead of rock.'

'I liked the caves,' smiled Anna.

'Good,' said Mum. 'Now let's find out how to get to the glacier.' She turned back to the notice. 'Oh! We need to go by the cable car that leaves from beside the *Hôtel de Neige*. I know where that is. Come on, *allez*!'

They marched off excitedly to the cable car and got there just as a large cabin lurched to a stop. Luckily there weren't many people waiting with them so they managed to squeeze onto it.

'This will be really cool!' remarked Kevin.

In fact he thought it was really terrifying. The cable car hurtled along, swinging and lurching in the wind. Between the tall pylons that supported it, the cabin seemed to lunge towards the ground before suddenly soaring up again.

'Oooh!' cried Kevin.

Tom tried to pretend he was enjoying the ride, but one look at his friend's white face showed him that Kevin was feeling just as scared as he was. Tom dropped all pretence and clung onto a rail in the cable car for dear life.

If Kevin and Tom looked white, then Mum was definitely green! Tom hoped she wasn't going to be sick over everyone. Anna, however, looked fine and chattered away merrily, not seeming to notice that no-one was listening to her.

At last the nightmare trip came to an end and they staggered out of the cable car at the top of the glacier. A sign pointed the way to the ice cave.

'I need to sit down,' said Mum shakily.

Kevin and Tom joined her as she perched on a rocky outcrop in the snow while Anna danced happily around the three of them. Soon Mum's face returned to its normal colour.

'Never, ever again,' she said firmly as they stood up. 'I just hope this cave is worth it!'

They started walking slowly beside the huge glacier. The boys knew that the enormous mass of ice was moving very, very slowly, but it looked so solid. And to think it had been formed by ordinary snowflakes that simply became crushed by the flakes falling on top of them, and so on, for thousands of years. It was incredible!

The cave itself was fantastic. It was quite expensive to get in. Tom expected Mum to make a fuss but she must have still been recovering from the journey in the cable car because she didn't say anything. Once inside, they were all speechless. To gaze around at the icy walls and the icy ceiling was fascinating. They could see the layers in the ice, and spot stones and even boulders that had been trapped in them. They slipped their gloves off and stroked the frozen walls until their fingers became numb. There was a strange light in the cave – not quite eerie, but certainly weird. And it was surprisingly warm. Tom had thought they would be absolutely frozen in the cave.

'Well, think about it,' said Kevin. 'Some Eskimos make their homes out of ice, don't they? They wouldn't do that if it meant they'd freeze to death. Being in this cave must be a bit like being in a giant igloo.'

Mum and the children stayed in the giant igloo for well over an hour before reluctantly heading back home for tea. Mum saw a sign pointing to a funicular railway that would take them back down to Grandmont. The cable car was completely out of the question!

As it turned out, the funicular railway was brilliant. The train, which looked like a staircase, consisted of lots of little compartments at different levels. The slope it travelled down was incredibly steep, but it was a slow and controlled descent. Halfway down the hill they passed another train coming up and the boys pulled faces and Anna waved at the passengers.

As they tramped back home from the funicular railway station, they passed the open-air ice rink.

'Can we have a really quick go, please, Mrs D?' begged Kevin.

'Goodness, where do you get all your energy from, Kevin?' asked Mum. 'I must be feeding you too much! Come on then, just for a while.'

Despite being pretty good on their inline skates, Tom and Kevin were hopeless on the ice.

'It's just too slippy!' protested Tom, as he crashed into the wall. His feet just wouldn't go in the direction he wanted them to.

Mum, however, was brilliant. She got off to a very wobbly start, but soon she was zooming around on the ice effortlessly.

'Cool, Mrs D!' called Kevin approvingly. Tom glowed with pride.

Even Anna had a go. They managed to hire a special pair of skates for her. She had a whale of a time crouching down and being pulled around on the ice by Mum.

After an hour of skating, falling, skating and crashing they gave back their skates and headed for home. All in all, a busy and energetic day.

6 Things Start Going Wrong

Mum was singing happily in the kitchen when the boys woke next morning.

'Uh, what's she got to be so happy about?' groaned Kevin, trying to summon up the enthusiasm to get out of his nice warm bed.

'Alan's coming today, silly,' explained Tom. 'Had you forgotten?'

'Do you think your Mum and Alan will get married?' asked Kevin.

Tom shrugged. 'I don't see how they can, since they live in different countries. They seem happy as they are.'

Something about Tom's tone made Kevin shoot a glance at him. Tom really liked Alan, Kevin knew, but he didn't seem keen on having him as part of the family. Kevin wondered if Tom was jealous or something. The truth was that Tom didn't want another Dad. He'd had the best dad in the world until he'd died suddenly, and a day didn't go by when he didn't think about him. Tom was happy to have Alan as a friend but nothing more.

'Hey, we've got our hike today!' called Kevin, changing the subject.

Tom's face cleared. 'Hey, cool. You'd better get up then, lazybones.' Tom grabbed his pillow and whacked Kevin with it. That started an energetic pillow fight that nearly got out of control but luckily Mum appeared at the right moment.

'Come on, you guys!' she warned, grabbing hold of both the pillows. 'Breakfast is ready. We've got a busy day ahead. You're hiking and Anna and I are collecting Alan. So scoot!'

An hour and a half later Mum left the two boys outside the ski school to start their day's hike. There were five other children, four of them about the same age as Kevin and Tom, and one kid who looked hardly older than Anna!

'He's a bit young, isn't he?' whispered Tom.

'Yeah, poor kid,' agreed Kevin. He walked over to the kid and smiled. 'Hi, I'm Kevin. This is my friend Tom. We're from Ireland.'

The young boy shot Kevin a startled look, but said nothing.

'Parlez-vous Anglais?' asked Tom.

The kid looked even more startled, and sidled away from them.

'Oh well,' shrugged Tom. 'At least we tried to be friendly.'

Just then, the guide turned up.

'Bonjour, je m'appelle Luc et . . . ' he rattled on in French. The boys couldn't understand a word. Eventually Luc paused and Tom saw his chance.

'Parlez-vous Anglais?' asked Tom hopefully.

'A little bit I only speak,' Luc replied with a sad shake of his head. He then carried on talking to the group in rapid French.

'Great!' muttered Kevin. 'How's your sign language, Tom?'

'We'll be OK,' said Tom. 'All we have to do is follow him anyway.'

Kevin nodded and they waited patiently until Luc had finished his long announcement.

'Allons-y! We go!' smiled Luc at the boys. And go they did, at quite a pace, with Luc striding out in front. Tom and Kevin had to trot to keep up with him, and that was hard work in the deep snow.

'Phew!' gasped Tom breathlessly, after they'd gone a mile or so. 'This is a killer!'

'You said it!' panted Kevin. 'I've got to stop for a second.' He came to a halt and breathed heavily for a moment.

Tom turned to see how far they'd come.

'Hey, Kevin!' he called. 'Look at that poor kid. He's miles behind us!'

Tom pointed to the tiny, struggling figure of the little boy in the snow a good few hundred metres behind them.

Kevin immediately shouted out to Luc to stop.

'Oy! Stop, er, *arrêtez. Attendez-nous*!' But Luc was too far ahead to hear them. 'What's with that guy?' complained Kevin. 'He's meant to be guiding us, not leaving us all behind. We're going to get lost.' Kevin looked worried.

'*Allez, vite!*' Tom called to the kid. The little boy caught up with them at last. He looked exhausted.

'Now, *donnez* your rucksack to *mon ami*,' Tom told him, 'and I'll give *vous* a hand.'

'Wow, my French must be improving,' grinned Kevin, 'because I understood that!'

Tom pulled a face at him. 'You do better then!' he challenged.

'I couldn't,' admitted Kevin. 'Come on, kid, give me the bag.' Kevin took the kid's rucksack and Tom took the boy by the hand. Then they staggered after the retreating Luc as quickly as possible.

'We'll never catch them!' exclaimed Kevin.

Just then, they were startled by the loud sound of an aeroplane engine. They glanced up and saw a small blue Cessna flying very low over them.

'It's very low,' observed Kevin.

It was, and suddenly it swooped even lower and the engine began to splutter.

'He's going to crash!' screamed Tom in fear.

The three boys watched in horror as the plane plunged into the mountain side above them.

'Quick, we must get help!' shouted Kevin. But his legs felt so wobbly from the shock of seeing the crash he wasn't sure he could move. One glance at Tom told him that his friend was as horrified as he was.

'*Non, non!*' shrilled the kid. They were the first words he'd said all day. '*Regardez!*' he shouted, pointing up the mountain.

Looking up, Tom and Kevin got an even bigger fright. Because sliding rapidly towards them was a huge wall of snow. The plane's impact had loosened a whole area. It was an avalanche!

7 Avalanche

For a split second, the boys couldn't believe their eyes. Then reality hit them and they sprang into action.

'Quick, let's get out of here!' cried Kevin.

'Yes, but where do we go?' demanded Tom. 'The avalanche is huge.'

They could feel the ground beneath their feet starting to shake as the rumbling wall of snow cascaded towards them.

Kevin felt on the edge of panic when suddenly the young kid tugged at his sleeve and pointed to a semi-circular outcrop of tall grey rocks about a hundred metres away.

'*Vite, vers les roches!*' he urged them.

'He's right, Tom,' called Kevin. 'Those rocks will shelter us. Come on, hurry.'

'Help me with the kid,'cried Tom.

Grabbing one arm of the kid each, the boys hurtled towards the rocks. Tom had never run so fast in his life. He usually trailed well behind Kevin but today they were neck and neck.

Closer and closer thundered the huge wave of snow. Would they make it to the rocks on time?

With only a split second to spare, the boys threw themselves onto the snow below the tall craggy rocks. As they lay there, snow exploded beside them and above them, but the rocks stopped the snow landing on them. The roar of the avalanche was deafening and the vibration almost threatened to roll the boys away from the rocks. But they clung tightly to each other and dug their feet into the snow and they stayed safe.

Suddenly it was all over. Tom looked up. They were now lying in a big hollow. The avalanche had deposited snow all around them but, thanks to the rocks, not on top of them.

'*Merci,*' said the kid in a shaky voice.

'Huh?' Tom was still stunned.

'*Merci,*' repeated the kid. 'Er, you save me!'

'*Eh . . . de rien,*' replied Kevin kindly. 'If you hadn't seen these rocks, well . . .' His voice trailed off as he contemplated what would have happened. 'I think we all sort of saved each other.'

Suddenly it was all too much. Kevin crumpled into a heap, with tears streaming down his face. Tom was by his side in an instant.

'Hey, Kev, stay cool!' he said, hugging his friend. 'We're OK! We'll be all right. But I'm not sure the others will be. We need to go and get help!'

Kevin sniffed, and wiped his eyes and nose on the back of his mittens.

'Yeah, you're right! Come on then.'

That was easier said than done. The three boys had to half climb, half burrow their way out of the hollow they now found themselves in. They were exhausted when they reached the surface and their mittens were soaking wet from digging snow.

They looked around. Nothing. They could see nothing – except snow and more snow. All the trees had disappeared, presumably either buried or torn out of the ground and dragged along by the avalanche. Nothing moved in the vast whiteness.

'The others must all have been buried alive!' cried Tom in dismay. 'We must go and get help.'

'Yes, but which way is help?' asked Kevin.

Kevin was right. Without any distinguishing landmarks, the expanse of snow that spread around them was completely disorientating.

'I guess we just head down, then,' shrugged Tom. He started down the hill slowly, falling into deep pockets of snow every so often.

'*Mais non, non,*' the kid suddenly piped up. '*Le pilote!* We, er 'elp him!'

'Golly, I'd forgotten about the pilot of the plane,' admitted Tom. 'The kid's right, he needs help too.'

'It was that idiot of a pilot who started this wretched avalanche in the first place,' Kevin reminded him. 'I don't feel sorry for him at all.'

'I know, but I'm sure he didn't mean to crash. And maybe his radio will still be working and then we could raise the alarm. The kid's right, Kev. We should try and find the pilot.'

'OK,' agreed Kevin. 'Up we go then!'

They turned round and began to struggle up the hillside through the deep snow. It seeped into their boots and made their socks and feet wet. But they battled on in the eerie quiet. Kevin was muttering some pretty rude things under his breath. They became even ruder when he suddenly bashed his foot against something hard in the snow.

'Yow!' he cried falling flat on his face in the snow.

'What's up, Kev?' Tom bent down to help his friend up.

49

'I bashed my foot on a rock or something and it hurts.' In rage, he began kicking at the hard object again. Snow flew into the air, revealing a chunk of something blue and metallic.

Tom stooped to look closer.

'Hey, hey, stop Kev, it's not a rock. It's blue, and it's made out of metal and . . . Jeepers! It's the plane. Kev, you're brilliant, you've found the plane!'

Tom flung himself onto his knees and began scrabbling in the snow. Kevin and the young kid started digging too. They cleared a lot more snow away. Without doubt, it was the small Cessna they had seen earlier that day.

'But how come it's here?' asked Kevin. 'I thought it crashed further up the mountain.'

'Maybe it was swept down with all the snow,' guessed Tom. 'Well, don't just sit there looking pleased with yourself! Help me dig! *Et vous*, kid! We've got to get the pilot out!'

'I hope he's still alive,' said Kevin anxiously.

'You're right,' said Tom. 'If his plane has tumbled halfway down the mountain, and then been buried in snow, the chances are he could be seriously hurt.'

They began digging again. Kevin remarked that he was glad he wasn't a rabbit or a mole who had to burrow all the time because digging was a pain. For the next while Tom, Kevin and the kid worked furiously in silence, pausing only to rest their arms when they started to ache.

They uncovered one of the wings and began to excavate the fuselage. It was very badly dented. Tom's stomach churned a bit at the thought of what they might find inside it. But just then the kid gave a cry. '*Un pied!*'

'A foot!' translated Tom. 'The kid's seen the pilot's foot.'

'But is it still attached to the pilot?' asked Kevin.

'We won't know till we look,' said Tom firmly. They quickly but carefully cleared away more snow from the black boot.

Soon they had uncovered the whole leg and eventually the rest of the pilot, who was lying twisted in the snow. Quite how he came to be lying outside the plane, the boys couldn't begin to fathom. But amazingly he didn't appear to be badly hurt. He had some bruises, and a couple of nasty gashes, but he was still breathing and looked a healthy shade of pink.

'What do we do now?' asked Kevin. 'I'm not very good at First Aid.'

Tom wasn't too hot either. 'Well, I don't think we should move him. We ought to try and warm him up, but what with?'

'Here, use my jacket,' said Kevin, thankfully pulling it off. 'I'm boiling alive with all this digging.'

'*Et moi aussi,*' added the kid, taking his coat off too. Tom joined them and they laid the coats over the pilot.

'Right, now let's see if we can find the radio and get it to work,' said Kevin.

They dug again. As they cleared snow from around the cockpit, first Tom and then Kevin came across several big heavy bundles of sticks that looked like marzipan. The sticks were wrapped in a sort of waxy paper. The kid had uncovered a few as well.

'Strange!' remarked Tom. 'Wonder what it is.'

The boys were mystified by the odd-looking bundles. Suddenly the kid got up and began to walk away from them.

'Hey, where's he going?' demanded Kevin.

Tom smiled. 'Use your imagination, Kev. It's hours since any of us have been to the loo!'

'Oh, yeah,' Kevin nodded wisely. 'Actually, that reminds me . . .'

'Turn round very slowly,' snapped a deep, gravelly voice.

Tom and Kevin gasped in fright. Instead of turning round slowly, they whipped round in alarm towards the voice. Then they froze. Sitting up in the snow behind them, and pointing a pistol at them, was the pilot.

'What . . . what . . .' Tom started to stammer.

'Shut up and you won't get hurt. Good, I see you speak English.' The pilot smiled nastily. 'Now, my two brave rescuers. I've got a job for you to do!'

'Two?' whispered Kevin to Tom. 'What about the kid?'

'Ssh!' said Tom. 'Don't say anything.'

'I told you to shut up!' snarled the pilot again. Tom gasped and stayed still. Obviously the kid had seen what was happening and nipped off before the pilot spotted him. Tom hoped the young boy would be all right on his own. But he couldn't worry about him right now – not when he and Kevin had a gun pointing at them. The pilot must be a madman or a criminal.

8 The Pilot

The pilot slowly and painfully stood up. He took a step towards Tom and Kevin and stooped to pick up one of the big bundles the boys had dug up. He gasped with pain as he tried to lift it and let it drop back into the snow.

'Here's the deal, kids,' he smirked. 'It seems I'm a bit the worse for my little accident.'

'Little accident?' Tom blurted out. 'That avalanche nearly killed us and you've probably killed loads of people who were out having fun.'

'So terribly sorry,' sighed the pilot insincerely. 'Now, back to my proposal. You two boys help me carry my precious bundles to my friend and I won't shoot you. How does that sound?'

'Wonderful,' replied Kevin sarcastically.

'Good. I see you were wearing rucksacks.' He glanced to where the boys had taken off their rucksacks. Tom hoped he wouldn't notice there were actually three of them. The kid was their only hope of being rescued now.

'Now, load up my bundles into your rucksacks and then we're going for a walk. My friend isn't very patient, and if I don't meet his deadline, then I'm a dead man. And so are you two, of course. Come on, move,' he shouted, waving the pistol menacingly.

'Sorry,' hissed Tom, as the boys knelt down to stuff the heavy bundles into their rucksacks. 'You were right, we shouldn't have bothered rescuing this guy. I've got us into this mess.'

'Don't be daft,' Kevin whispered back. 'How were we to know he'd turn out to be some kind of homicidal maniac. Your idea to use the radio in the plane was a good one. Hang in there, buddy!'

But Tom's misery was clearly etched on his tired face. They were really in trouble this time.

'Come on, move it!' snapped the pilot.

'We're going as fast as we can!' retorted Kevin, his cheeks burning with anger. It was hard stuffing the awkward bundles into the rucksacks, especially as his hands were shaking with a mixture of fear and rage. 'Anyway, what is this stuff?'

'Never you mind. Let's just say that it's very valuable, so no messing. Now get on with it!'

The pilot stepped closer to them, with a threatening look on his face. The boys worked faster.

'What do you think it is, then?' hissed Kevin.

'Well, I don't think it's marzipan,' replied Tom grimly, 'although that's what the stuff looks like. I reckon it's dynamite or something.'

'Crikey! Will it go off?' gasped Kevin.

'No, I don't think so. Most explosives are pretty stable until you add the detonator,' Tom quickly reassured him. 'We'll be OK.'

'Shut up!' said the pilot. 'Little boys should be seen and not heard. Now, are you ready? Good, let's move!' came the order.

Kevin and Tom quickly covered the third rucksack with snow and staggered to their feet. They were tired enough after the day's adventures, but now they had to carry heavy rucksacks on their backs on top of everything else!

'No, wait a minute,' said the pilot, motioning to them to put the rucksacks down. 'How silly of me. One more job to do. Fill in those large holes you dug in the snow around the plane.'

Tom and Kevin looked at each other in surprise.

'Why?' asked Kevin.

'Just do it,' snarled the pilot. 'I don't like kids who ask questions. Still, if you must know, if you fill in the holes then when any rescuers come along they'll think I'm still buried in the snow. They'll spend a nice long time looking for me. Meanwhile, we get further away. Now do it!'

The pilot sat down in the snow a few metres behind them, watching them and pointing his pistol at them.

The boys bent down and began shovelling back all the snow they had so painstakingly dug out not long ago.

'He's completely nuts!' whispered Tom while they worked. 'People will see our tracks out of here and guess that he's been rescued, surely!'

'You're right,' Kevin whispered back. 'But to make extra sure, I'll leave my Man United scarf. Not many pilots wear them I bet. If someone sees it, perhaps they'll guess that other people have been here too.'

'It'll help identify us too,' nodded Tom. 'Especially if Mum comes looking for us. Oh boy, she's going to be frantic when she hears about the avalanche.' Tom was close to tears.

'Hey, she knows we're survivors!' said Kevin, trying to comfort him. 'Didn't we escape a volcano in the summer, *and* find our way through a cave system!'

Tom managed a thin smile. 'Yeah, you're right. We're survivors!' he agreed.

The holes were just about filled in.

'Distract him for a minute,' whispered Kevin.

'Hey!' called Tom, turning towards the pilot. 'Didn't I hear an engine?' He stood up and peered into the sky.

'What?' the pilot jumped up. 'Not already? I thought it would be a bit longer before the search planes came up. There might be the risk of starting another avalanche if they came so soon.'

The pilot anxiously scanned the blue skies. While he did that, Kevin pulled off his favourite scarf, laid it on the ground and pushed one end firmly into the snow to anchor it. Then he and Tom grabbed the rucksacks and took a few paces away from where it was buried.

'OK, I've done it,' whispered Kevin.

The pilot turned round to face them again. 'Stupid kid,' he sneered. 'Nothing there. Finished? Good, let's march.'

The three set off, looking like a sorry crowd. In front were Tom and Kevin, tired and overloaded. Behind them was the pilot, bruised and battered after his crash. He limped and hobbled along, frequently slipping, but he never lost his grip on the gun.

How are we going to get out of this one? thought Tom.

9 Where's Alan?

Mum and Anna arrived at the train station in good spirits. The boys were having a good time, or so she thought, Anna was her usual happy self and Mum was certainly looking forward to seeing Alan again. Now the holiday would really start for her.

They were early – Mum always got to places like stations and airports way too early – so they browsed in the newsagent's shop on the station concourse and then had a snack at the café.

Mum checked her watch.

'Five to one!' she smiled. 'Five minutes till Alan's train arrives at platform three. Let's go.'

They sauntered over to the platform and waited for a while. Five minutes passed, and then another five.

'Where's Alan?' asked Anna eventually. She was getting bored of peering down the empty track.

'Good question,' replied Mum. 'I'd like to know where he is too! The train's been delayed for some reason. We'll just have to be patient.'

But Anna wasn't feeling patient. She started being naughty and Mum got ratty.

'Oh, just behave, why can't you!' she said crossly as Anna started swinging on a piece of railing and accidentally kicked several passers-by in the process. 'I don't want to be all het up when Alan gets here.'

But after another quarter of an hour, Mum was very het up. She hated hanging around and wasting time like this. Where was Alan's train?

Just then, a voice crackled over the loudspeaker system. Mum didn't catch much of it but she heard the words '*St Hilaire*' and '*avalanche*'.

'Hey! St Hilaire! That's where Alan's train is coming from. And wasn't there something about an avalanche!' Mum looked worried. Seeing her expression, Anna started behaving herself. 'Oh, I wish my French was better,' Mum exclaimed.

'Hey, what's the problem? Maybe I can help?' came a voice in an American accent. Mum looked up at the tall, young man who stood by her side. 'My French is pretty darn good, though I say so myself!' he grinned.

'I was wondering what that last announcement was all about. I'm waiting for a friend of mine.

He's due to arrive on the St Hilaire train, and I'm sure I heard something about an avalanche.'

'You sure did,' replied the American. 'There's been a real big avalanche near Grandmont and it's caused a few smaller ones further away. One of those has blocked the line a little way from here and that's what's holding up the train.'

'Grandmont? An avalanche at Grandmont?'

'Are you OK?' he asked as Mum turned white.

'Oh no,' cried Mum. 'That's where Tom and Kevin have gone hiking today. I have to get back. Come on, Anna, we need to get back to the boys!'

Mum grabbed Anna's hand and started to pull her along the platform back towards the car park.

'But what about Alan!' wailed Anna.

'Alan will understand when he finds out,' said Mum. 'Oh, thank you!' she called back over her shoulder to the American man.

'Any time, ma'am!' he shouted back, looking slightly puzzled.

Mum began to run.

'Mummy, you're going too fast!' screamed Anna, starting to cry.

'Oh, I'm sorry, angel,' panted Mum, stopping and lifting her up. 'I forgot about your little legs.

I'm very worried about the boys. We must get back to Grandmont as quickly as we can.'

Anna was puzzled, but sensed that Mum was feeling scared about something so she just clung on tight as Mum jogged determinedly towards their little hired car. Mum plonked Anna down and fumbled for the keys in her handbag with shaking hands.

'Stay calm! Stay calm!' she told herself firmly. 'The boys will be fine. They'll be fine.'

But she wasn't convinced. Her precious family had escaped a disaster once already this year. Maybe their luck was running out.

Mum was a great driver – considerate, careful and law-abiding. But not today! On the way back she became as French as the rest of the road users, hooting at even the briefest of delays in the traffic ahead, cutting in front of cars at junctions and jumping lights. She wasn't quite reckless – not with little Anna as a passenger – but she came pretty close.

'Just pray we don't meet a gendarme!' she cried to Anna. Anna wondered briefly who John Darm was but soon went back to watching the world rush by at an unaccustomed speed.

Before long, Mont Glace reared up before them with Grandmont nestled at its foot.

'Nearly there!' cried Mum. She pushed the accelerator right down to the floor for the last few kilometres. She screeched to a halt outside the apartment on the outskirts of town.

'*Now* what do I do?' Mum suddenly thought. She realised that she hadn't been thinking at all on the journey back from the station. It was as though instinct had taken over. She knew she had to get back quickly, but without really knowing why.

'Come on, come on, pull yourself together!' Mum muttered.

'Pair of curtains joke!' smiled Anna, hearing Mum's words. The 'Doctor, doctor, I think I'm a pair of curtains' joke was one of Tom's favourites.

Anna's voice brought Mum back to earth.

'That's right, Anna dear,' she managed to smile. 'Now, we must go up to the ski school and see if we can find out exactly what's going on. It's just a few minutes' walk.'

They set off at as brisk a pace as Anna could manage. Just as Mum was beginning to wonder why she hadn't had the sense to drive up to the ski school, they turned a corner and stopped. The road ahead of them was completely jammed with cars. A lot of people had decided to go to the ski school to find out about their friends and family who had been out on the mountain when the avalanche had occurred.

Mum's heart sank. She lifted Anna again and hurried on. The pavements were thronged with people, talking together at the tops of their voices. It was chaos.

Just then Mum caught sight of an elderly English woman she'd spoken to at the ice rink.

'What's happening, Margaret?' she asked her desperately.

The woman turned. 'Oh Jane, dear! My daughter and her husband were skiing!' was all she could say, tears streaming down her face.

'My son and his friend were out there too!' replied Mum, fighting back her own tears. Crying wouldn't do any good, she told herself angrily.

Mum and Anna waited for a few minutes, trying to understand what the French people around them were saying. Mum could see it would be impossible for her to battle her way through to the front of the queue and speak to someone at the ski school. She was beginning to panic.

Mum glanced up at the sky for a moment. It was beautifully clear and blue. Who would have thought something so awful could happen on such a beautiful day? It was an even nicer day today than the one when they'd gone flying with André, Mum thought idly.

Suddenly she gasped. Of course! André! The altiport! Why hadn't she thought of it before? Maybe André would be there today, but even if he wasn't, surely they'd be sending out rescue flights soon. And at the moment, anything was better than standing around in a hysterical crowd.

'Where now?' asked Anna, as Mum heaved her up again and began jogging as fast as she could through the crowds.

'Up to the altiport. We'll try and find André,' Mum informed her.

People were still pouring towards the ski school. Mum and Anna were the only people going in the opposite direction.

On their way back they passed close to their apartment building. Mum paused for a second.

'Wait. We'd better just nip into the apartment for a moment,' she decided. 'We need to put our hiking boots on, and I want to leave a note for

Alan. He knows our address, so I'm sure he'll make his way here eventually when he sees we're not at the station.'

'I'm hungry!' observed Anna.

'OK,' Mum smiled. 'We'll raid the fridge too.'

10 Alan Arrives at Last

Mum felt better now for having a plan. She plonked Anna down and they hurried upstairs to their apartment. Once inside, Mum dug out some tasty chocolate biscuits for Anna and popped a few extra chocolate bars in the pockets of her coat for later. Anna was amazed. Mum usually carefully rationed the amount of chocolate she let them eat. This must be some sort of special occasion!

Mum found her sturdy hiking boots and then crammed her rucksack with all the emergency-related items she could think of – binoculars, a torch, more chocolate, spare socks, a compass, a map and a length of washing line she found in the cupboard under the sink. Quite what she might need these things for, she didn't know but it was comforting to feel prepared. She had just about finished when there was a knock at the door.

Mum rushed to answer it, hoping it might be the boys. But it wasn't. It was a sombre looking gendarme. Mum's heart sank into her boots.

'Have . . . Have you found them?' she asked tremulously. By 'them' she meant their bodies.

'*Et*, you are Mrs Donoghue?' The Frenchman pronounced every letter in her surname carefully.

Mum nodded.

'*Malheureusement*, I am sorry to say your boys are missing on the mountain. Search parties are ready to set off, but we need to be sure there is no more risk of avalanches, you understand?' he went on.

Mum just about did, despite the very heavy French accent the gendarme had.

The gendarme's eye fell on Mum's rucksack. '*Mais*, you are not thinking of going out to search yourself, I hope?'

'Heavens no!' Mum fibbed. 'I never unpacked this from our walk yesterday.'

Anna looked at Mum in horror. She'd never known Mum to tell a lie before.

'*Bon*,' said the gendarme. 'Because it is still dangerous out there. You must leave this to the experts. Here is the phone number of the gendarmerie. Please ring any time. We will contact you when we have news. *Au revoir.*' He turned and trudged down the hallway.

Mum shut the door and met Anna's accusing stare.

'You told the policeman lies,' she said.

'No I didn't, not really,' Mum defended herself. 'He said "I hope you weren't thinking of going out to search." Well, I'm not *thinking* of doing it – I'm *going* to do it. That's completely different.'

'OK, Mum.' Anna was satisfied.

Mum zipped them both into their warmest coats, allowing time for the gendarme to leave the building.

'OK,' she smiled to Anna. 'Off we go to find our boys!'

Just then, another loud knock on the door rang out.

'Oh no, he's come back!' thought Mum. She ripped off her coat and chucked the rucksack under the kitchen table, out of sight. Then she unceremoniously bundled Anna into the bathroom since there wasn't time to take off her coat.

'Stay there!' she hissed.

Mum hurried to the door and flung it open.

'Yes?' she asked crossly, glancing over her shoulder to check the bathroom door which was starting to open.

'Well, that's a fine welcome, I must say!' came the familiar voice of Alan.

'Alan!' Mum gasped with surprise and flung herself into his arms. Anna came charging out of the bathroom and wriggled between them to join in the hug.

'I thought you were the gendarme again,' she explained sheepishly.

'Are the boys missing then?' asked Alan concerned. 'I heard all about the avalanche on Mont Glace.'

'Yes, they . . .' but Mum's voice trailed away. Suddenly all the fear she had been trying to control got the better of her and the tears came thick and fast.

'Oh Alan, they're buried in the snow. We've got to find them.' Anna began to cry too, so for the next couple of minutes Alan hugged them both again and dried tears and blew noses.

'Anyway,' said Mum, recovering a little. 'How come you're here so quickly? We thought you were stuck on your train so we came back.'

'I was stuck!' smiled Alan. 'We were told that the avalanche had blocked the line and that we would have to wait until it was all cleared away.

It's weird, but I got this really strange feeling that you guys were in trouble. I just couldn't stay on the train, so I jumped off and hiked through the snow till I came to a road. Then I hitched my way to Grandmont. Thanks to these maniac French drivers, I got here in no time.'

'Thank goodness you're here,' sighed Mum. 'But you just caught us in time. I was about to head off to the altiport. I've met up with André, the person I used to be an au pair for years ago, and he's got a plane up at the altiport. I was going up to see if I could get him to fly me over the mountain to look for the boys. Now you're here, can you mind Anna while I go? I'd rather not be dragging her out.'

Alan could see clearly from Mum's determined expression that there was only one possible answer to her question.

'Yes, of course I'll hold the fort. There should be someone here in case there's any news from the gendarmerie. But do take care, Jane.'

'I will. I'll find my precious boys, you'll see.'

She kissed Alan and Anna, put her coat on and heaved the rucksack onto her back.

'See you later,' she smiled. Then she was gone.

11 Searching

Mum sprinted to the altiport. It was a long way and her pack was heavy but she took no notice. The only time she faltered was when she thought she saw a figure up ahead. Fearful that it might be the gendarme, she ducked down behind a bank of snow. She scrabbled in the rucksack and pulled out the binoculars. She allowed herself a brief proud smile for packing them in the first place. She trained the binoculars on the movement up ahead and saw to her relief that it was a deer!

In no time she was back on the path and moments later she panted up to the altiport. She raced for the little radio room and waiting room André had shown them the other day. To her delight, André was there, together with two other pilots.

'André, thank goodness!' she exclaimed.

'*Eh, voilà*. You see?' André grinned to his colleagues. 'Women, they are always so glad to see me!'

His friends chuckled.

'Jane, what can I do for you?' he asked as he came forward to kiss Mum's cheek.

'André, you've got to take me up in your plane. I need to find the boys!'

'What!' gasped André in horror. 'Your boys were out in the avalanche? *Mon Dieu!* But Jane, I am so sorry, I cannot fly. We are not allowed to go up in case we start another avalanche. We are waiting to get permission to go and help with the search. As soon as the clearance comes through, we will begin seeking for survivors.'

Mum sank onto a nearby chair. Suddenly all her strength was gone.

'But André, my son is out there! I've just got to find him. Can't you go now? Wouldn't you want to find Alexandre if he were missing?' she wailed.

André only needed to think about his own son for a split second before he realised the full anguish Mum was going through. He pulled his headset on and called up ground control. Luckily his old friend Albert was on duty and André explained the problem. Mum couldn't understand what he was saying, but it sounded very persuasive! At last, his face cracked into a broad grin.

'*Merci, mon brave!*' he chuckled.

He pulled off the headset and hurried towards the door.

'We have permission to go, but I must stay above a certain height, otherwise I am in big trouble,' he explained to Mum.

'Oh thank you, André. I can't tell you how grateful I am,' said Mum with relief.

André went through his pre-flight checks while Mum climbed into the cockpit. Then André heaved himself in beside her and started the engine. Within minutes they were trundling out onto the runway. As the plane sprinted towards the end of the airstrip, Mum saw the huge drop below and it was almost too much for her. She closed her eyes tightly.

'You won't be much of a lookout,' joked André.

Mum opened her eyes cautiously. She gasped at the view below her. She stopped feeling nervous at once.

'If I wasn't so worried about the boys, I could really enjoy this,' she said.

'Me too,' said André. 'Now, where was their hike taking them?'

'I don't know,' admitted Mum. 'It was an eight-kilometre mountain hike leaving from the ski school.'

'*Mais oui*, those guided hikes. They usually head towards Les Aguilles – that's a narrow ridge of rock on the west slope of Mont Glace. I think we will start there.'

André spoke into his headset to the control tower and then changed course. The plane banked steeply. Mum gripped her seat tightly as they swerved round!

'I will go as low as I am allowed,' said André, quickly losing altitude. The orange needle on the dial raced round and round. Mum held on tightly to her seat again.

'OK, this is as low as we can go,' said André. '*Regardez bien!*'

He didn't need to tell Mum to keep a sharp lookout. She was already scouring the snow below them for any sign of life. There was nothing to be seen.

But suddenly Mum spotted a black dot ahead. Then several black dots.

'André, I see something!' she called excitedly. 'About ten o'clock.' She pointed as well.

André steered towards the dots.

'*Ah, oui!* I see them. *Combien*? Four or five I think?'

'Hm, but that's not enough,' replied Mum, worried. 'There were seven of them plus the guide, so that group can't be the boys' hiking party. Unless some are missing of course.'

They flew on towards the group. Mum could just make out the hike leader. It *was* their group! But there was no sign of the boys.

'That's their party all right,' she said to André tearfully as they flew past. 'But Tom and Kevin aren't there!'

'Maybe they just got split up. Don't give up hope, Jane,' André squeezed her hand. '*Attendez.* I will radio in their position so someone can pick them up.'

He spoke into his headset again, and then changed course. 'Now we search further north,' he told Mum. The plane banked once more.

Mum blinked back the tears as she strained her eyes staring in every direction for the boys, but all she could see was snow. Where, oh where could they be? Please let them be safe, she prayed to herself.

'Hey, I see something!' exclaimed André, making Mum jump. '*La-bàs!* A single figure! We'll go down just a little lower.'

Mum looked. Yes, there did appear to be a black dot on the snow. But only one. Could it be either Kevin or Tom? She looked more closely. No, it seemed to be a very young child. Mum didn't know it, but the young child was 'the kid'. He waved frantically at the plane and kept pointing to the east.

'I think he's trying to tell us something,' said Mum. 'Go that way, André.'

André once more radioed co-ordinates to the control tower, this time to tell them the young boy's position.

'I wonder what *le petit garçon* wants us to find?' murmured André, changing course again.

Mum scanned the horizon for any sign of, well – anything!

'I can't see them yet, André,' she sighed. 'Wait a minute. I'm not sure, but look over there. It looks like a sort of shadow in the snow. There are lots of footprints too by the looks of it,' said Mum hopefully. 'But I don't see anyone.'

'*Allons-y.* Just a tiny bit lower,' grinned André.

The draught from the propellers caused the snow to swirl about on the ground below them. The snow was blown away to reveal a bright red patch with a few tiny splashes of yellow.

'No, it can't be . . . yes, it's a Man Utd scarf!' exclaimed Mum.

'A *quoi* scarf?' asked André puzzled.

'Man Utd, a football team,' explained Mum. 'That's Kevin's scarf, it has to be. He's mad about that team. Kevin has been here, I know it!'

A wave of relief flooded over her. It looked as though the boys were OK. If Kevin was around here somewhere, then Tom wouldn't be far away. Those boys were practically inseparable.

André circled round again.

'I think there is something buried in the snow,' he said. 'It has been badly covered up. Maybe this is where the plane that caused the avalanche came down.'

'Oh, I didn't know a plane had caused it!' replied Mum, surprised.

'Yes, it was a plane owned by an Englishman, Samuel Raymonds. He is not *très agréable*, this Mr Raymonds. Several of the pilots, they think he is up to no good,' André went on.

'Why? Crime of some sort?' suggested Mum.

'They don't know, nor do I, but he is up to something. Look, there is a kind of trail in the snow there, see? I will follow it.' André swerved away from the buried plane.

'There, I see something moving!' cried Mum a few moments later. 'One, two, three people. They seem to be running!'

'*Oui,* I see!' said André. 'Down a bit lower – I will be shot for doing this!' he pulled a face.

'I'll never tell Albert on you,' smiled Mum. Her spirits were rising all the time. She was sure it was the boys up ahead. There was something very familiar about them, even at this distance.

André swooped towards the people. They kept running away, for some reason. Then suddenly one of them, the tallest, swung round and raised an arm towards the plane. There was a sudden sharp bang on the nose of the plane and then an almighty crunch as the windscreen cracked.

'*Mon Dieu!*' yelled André. '*C'est impossible.* He is shooting at us!'

Mum ducked as André hauled back on the stick and the little Cherokee climbed steeply.

'And I was only joking when I said I'd get shot for flying so low,' protested André.

A couple more sharp bangs on the belly of the plane told them they were still being fired at. Mum raised her head enough to look out of the plane. She saw Tom and Kevin's terrified faces staring up at her. She waved but couldn't tell if they'd seen her.

André was jabbering madly into his headset while he checked his various dials. Mum saw him looking at one in particular with concern. It looked like the fuel gauge. The needle was dropping sharply. Mum picked out words like 'pistolet', 'gendarmes' and 'Monsieur Raymonds' from André's rapid conversation with the control tower. At last André finished and turned to her, an anxious expression on his face.

'We must go back,' he explained. 'The plane is damaged and we are losing fuel. The gendarmes will take over the search. Your boys will be OK.'

'Go back!' Mum felt helpless again.

During the search at least she had felt she was doing something. Now she would have to sit back and wait for someone else to get things done.

'Don't worry, Jane,' said André reassuringly. 'You will all be together soon.'

12 Tying Up Loose Ends

Down on the snow, the boys watched as the plane flew away. They were delighted when they first saw it as they had recognised André's little Cherokee. Tom was sure he'd seen Mum in the plane too. They were horrified when the pilot fired at the plane, throwing themselves down onto the ground when they heard the shots. Tom's heart was still pounding from the fright. His legs felt all wobbly too. But the plane didn't appear to be damaged so Mum and André were safe.

'It was Mum and André!' hissed Tom as they lay in the snow.

'They'll get help,' Kevin whispered back.

The pilot was furious. He swore and kicked at the snow with his good leg.

'Come on, come on!' he screamed at the boys. 'We must hurry. This place will be crawling with rescue parties soon, blast it!'

The pistol was pointing at them again, so the boys had no choice but to do as they were told.

The Englishman was really annoyed. Kevin got up and started to pull his rucksack on, but Tom slipped and fell.

'Ouch! My ankle!' Tom cried, rubbing where it hurt. Kevin went over to his friend.

'Oh, don't try that trick,' snarled the pilot. 'You're not hurt. Now get up or else!'

'I can't!' protested Tom. 'I really did hurt my ankle. I don't think I can stand.'

'You'll stand, kid,' shouted the pilot. He aimed a vicious kick at Tom's leg. Tom yelled with pain. That was too much for Kevin.

'Leave my friend alone, you bully!' He lunged at the pilot and tackled him, luckily before he could shoot. They fell in the snow, struggling and kicking. Then Kevin realised that the pilot had stopped moving. He had hit his head on a boulder hidden just below the surface of the snow.

'Wow, I think you've killed him, Kev!' said Tom. 'You must have pushed him against that rock.'

'Oh no,' gasped Kevin, turning white. 'I don't want to go to prison.'

Then the pilot groaned.

'Phew. He's OK!' sighed Kevin with relief.

'You wouldn't have gone to prison, anyway,' said Tom. 'You were defending us. Thanks for saving me, Kev. You're a true friend.'

'He made me so angry when he kicked you. Are you OK?' Kevin crouched down next to his friend who was rubbing both his legs now.

'Pretty sore. But look, he'll come round soon. We've got to tie him up.' Tom was practical as ever. 'And we must take his gun away.'

'There it is,' said Kevin, spotting it in the snow where the pilot had dropped it when he fell. Kevin picked up the gun very, very carefully. 'Cool! I've never held a gun before.'

'Just don't point it at me please,' said Tom.

'What am I supposed to do with it?' asked Kevin. 'It's kind of scary holding it actually.'

'Better put it in one of the rucksacks on its own, I guess,' suggested Tom. 'Now, let's tie up this guy before he wakes up.'

'What with?' wondered Kevin.

'Anything we can find. Here, let's use his belt and bootlaces for a start.'

Tom shuffled on his bottom up to the pilot. His ankle felt too sore to stand up just yet.

'If we leave him here, won't he get frostbite?' asked Kevin, tugging the pilot's belt off.

'You're full of concern for the guy all of a sudden, considering you just nearly killed him,' teased Tom as he began to untie the bootlaces.

'You're right, he deserves to get frostbite.'

Tom pulled off his scarf and wrapped it tightly round one of the pilot's wrists. Then he heaved both the man's arms behind his back and tied them tightly together using the scarf and the bootlaces. He did triple and quadruple reef knots.

Meanwhile, Kevin was tightening the belt around the pilot's legs. He added his own belt too for extra security. I just hope these hold! he thought to himself.

'There, that should do!' exclaimed Kevin, standing up and admiring his handiwork. 'We'd better scarper before he comes to properly. Give me your hand, Tom, I'll help you up.'

Tom grabbed Kevin's hand and cautiously pulled himself up. His ankle was really throbbing but he could just about put his weight on it.

'I'm OK, Kev!' he grinned. 'Let's take the gun with us and keep one of these sticks of dynamite to show the gendarmes – when we find them.'

'Which way do you think we should go?' asked Kevin.

'Any way, so long as it's away from him,' Tom nodded to the pilot. 'Let's go the same way André's plane flew off. That must have been towards the altiport.'

'Good thinking,' said Kevin.

They set off walking as quickly as Tom could manage.

'I hope that little kid's OK,' panted Tom as he limped alongside Kevin. 'I wonder where he got to when he ran off?'

'Yeah, and all the others in the hiking party,' said Kevin. 'I hope they didn't get buried in that awful avalanche.' He glanced back over his shoulder at the pilot. 'That madman's still out cold,' he reassured Tom. 'Hey, out cold. That was a pun. Did you get it?'

Tom nodded and managed a little grin. Then he stopped in his tracks.

'Look, look!' Tom shouted, pointing ahead. 'Is that Luc and the others?

'Where?'

'See, down there near the trees, there's a group of people.'

Kevin peered into the distance.

'Golly, you've sure got laser eyesight, Tom,' he said admiringly. 'I can't really see anything. No, hang on! I see them. And aren't those dogs too? Hey, it must be rescuers!'

'Now who's got the laser eyesight!' grinned Tom. 'I never saw the dogs. Hey, they're running towards us!'

'Good dogs! Come up here and rescue us!' called Kevin.

The dogs came streaking across the snow towards them.

'They're going really fast for St Bernards!' observed Kevin.

'They're not St Bernards, Kev. They look like Alsatians!' remarked Tom, stopping. 'And they don't look very friendly.'

'Crikey, you're right!' agreed Kevin. There was certainly something menacing about the way the dogs were running with silent determination towards them.

'Let's run!' yelped Kevin.

But it was too late. The next instant the air around them seemed to fill with dark fur and sharp teeth. Tom felt something heavy grabbing his arm.

He was pulled down to the ground and became aware of a weight on his chest. He shook the snow out of his eyes and looked up. Six inches from his face were the slobbering jaws of a huge brown Alsatian. Tom rolled his eyes and glanced across to where Kevin was flat on his face a few feet away – with another dog sitting on him!

'Hey!' protested Kevin. 'I thought you were meant to be rescued by dogs in the mountains, not sat on by them!'

Tom started to giggle, despite the crazy circumstances. But the dog standing on him didn't like that and growled menacingly at him.

'These definitely aren't rescue dogs, Kev!' observed Tom. 'Here come their handlers now. I hope they're good guys!'

Three men were hurrying over. As they came closer, Tom could see they were gendarmes. But they had their pistols out, pointing at the boys.

'Well, they *are* good guys,' he informed Kevin, 'but they look like they want to shoot us. What did we do wrong today?' The dog growled again.

'I don't know, but I think we'll find out soon,' said Kevin.

The gendarmes panted up to them.

'*Mais, ce sont les enfants!*' one called in surprise, staring down at the boys. He snapped out an order and the dogs jumped lightly off Tom and Kevin, and sat down wagging their tails.

The gendarme helped the boys get up.

'*Alors!* We thought you were bad persons,' he explained apologetically. 'My colleagues have just arrested a smuggler of explosives we have been watching for a long time. With a little persuasion he told them that he was expecting a delivery of dynamite by plane today, except that the plane crashed into the mountain. The pilot sent him a radio message as his plane was going down. We set out to intercept with our, er, sniffer dogs. But they find you two! It is strange!' He shook his head perplexed.

'No, no, it's not strange!' burst out Kevin, jumping up and down in excitement. 'Your sniffer dogs are brilliant. The pilot made us carry his dynamite. We must reek of it. No wonder the dogs sat on us! Look, there's some in Tom's rucksack. And I've got the pilot's gun in mine.' Kevin began rummaging in the rucksacks to pull out their treasures.

'And the pilot is up the hill over there,' added Tom, pointing up the slope. 'We dug him out of his plane but then he turned a gun on us. Kevin knocked him out when he kicked me and then we tied him up. Quickly, get him before he escapes. I don't know how good our knots are!'

'This is true?' the gendarme looked impressed. He turned to his colleagues and ordered them to find the pilot. They set off with the dogs.

Kevin laid the pistol and the parcels of dynamite on the snow in front of the gendarme, who then whistled softly.

'*Très bien,*' he said admiringly.

Then he pulled out a walkie-talkie.

'*Vite!* Tell me your names and I will tell the rescue centre that you are safe. I expect your parents are worried.'

'Mine won't be!' said Kevin brightly. 'They're in Ireland.'

Tom saw the gendarme's puzzled look so he quickly piped up: 'I'm Tom Donoghue and this is Kevin Murphy. My mum is Jane Donoghue and she's staying at the Grand Place apartments. Mind you, she's probably at the altiport because she went up in a plane to find us.'

The gendarme looked even more puzzled now, but he nodded and relayed the information to the rescue centre down at the ski school. His face cleared a little while he was speaking.

He turned to the boys again. '*Ah, oui, c'est ça.* I understand, yes. A plane with your mother and a man called André radioed in your position. Several rescuers are already on the way on foot. They will take you back to base. The helicopter is not allowed to land in the mountains today in case of another avalanche.'

Kevin looked disappointed.

'Don't you want to be rescued, Kev?' Tom asked.

'Yes, of course, but I really fancied being winched up in a helicopter,' he explained.

'Me too,' agreed Tom. 'But at least we can walk, well, hobble back to safety. I bet there are people who've been badly hurt. They will probably have to be airlifted from the altiport.'

'You're right, as usual,' said Kevin, a little shamefaced.

'Hey, that reminds me,' said Tom turning to the gendarme. 'There's a little kid, I mean, a boy wandering around here somewhere on his own.

And a group of some hikers too. Can you tell the rescuers about them?'

The gendarme spoke into his walkie-talkie again. He was nodding his head as he listened.

'*Le petit garçon et les autres?* They were all spotted by your mother and her pilot friend,' he told them a few moments later. 'They'll be picked up soon.'

'Thank goodness!' sighed Tom.

'Will our rescuers have St Bernards with them?' asked Kevin. He was determined to have some dramatic aspect to his rescue.

'*Mais oui*, I expect, yes,' agreed the gendarme. Suddenly his walkie-talkie crackled into life again. He listened, replied, and then looked up.

'My colleagues have found your pilot,' he informed the boys, smiling. 'Apparently he is very angry and all tied up with belts and bootlaces. Well done, *mes garçons!* Now, I must organise some reinforcements to take the pilot away.'

He returned to his walkie-talkie.

Tom sighed and sank back in the deep snow. The next half hour or so passed in a bit of a daze. First more gendarmes arrived on the scene and frogmarched the pilot off to the gendarmerie.

Next some paramedics arrived on skis and checked Tom and Kevin out. They bandaged Tom's bad ankle up. And then, finally, Kevin's long awaited St Bernards bounded up with a mountain rescue team who then escorted the boys over to the altiport where Mum, Alan and Anna were waiting.

That was quite some reunion!

13 Together At Last

Later that night, they sat around a table in the 'best restaurant' in Grandmont, McDonald's. The day's excitement was almost over. The last few missing people had all been found. Amazingly, no one had been killed by the avalanche although there were some nasty injuries.

And a notorious explosives dealer and his pilot were behind bars, thanks to the boys. Tom and Kevin had given full statements to the police. Afterwards, journalists and photographers had come and gone to their Mont Glace apartment to get the full story. The boys were heroes and they were looking forward to seeing their names in the papers the next day.

Now they were having a quiet supper – well, as quiet as it could be with three over-excited and over-tired children, two relieved adults and the setting of a busy fast-food restaurant.

'All I want to know is why *can't* we be a nice, normal family having a nice, normal holiday?' groaned Mum, toying with her last tasty chip.

She felt completely drained from the mixture of emotions – horror, worry, hope, despair and relief – that she'd endured that day.

'I was just thinking the same thing,' smiled Alan. 'But then, I wouldn't love you all as much as I do!'

'Can I have another burger?' asked Kevin. 'I'm still starving. Escaping from avalanches and catching villains is hungry work!'

'Mmm! Me too,' said Tom, winking at his friend. Alan stuffed several twenty franc notes into Kevin's hand.

'Get lots!' he ordered. 'You deserve them!'

'Cool!' said Kevin gratefully and trotted up to the counter.

'Mum,' said Tom thoughtfully.

'Yes, Tom.'

'When this holiday is over, where will the next one be?'

Mum raised an eyebrow. '*If* there is a next one,' she replied with a smile. 'We still haven't finished this one yet . . .'